This book belongs to ...

_____

www.HankTheOutdoorsman.com

Hank the Outdoorsman

Deer Hunting with Dad

Written By
Josh Ishmael

Illustrated by
Brian Azhar

Dad is a hunter,
so is Grandpa Joe.
When I get older,
I can't wait to go

Nov 10, 1980.
Spencer And Joe headed out for the hunt

Dad goes hunting
When it's hot or cold,
Grandpa doesn't go much,
He is getting old.

With the wind from the east
and snow in his face,
Dad sat down in his favorite place.

20 feet in the air, high in the stand
Tonight, Dad only saw land!

As I left from school
it was chilly and gray,
I figured that I would just
Go home and play.

As I got to the house Dad's truck
Was parked out front.
He asked me if I wanted to go hunt!

We packed all the gear
in the back of the truck.
I prayed tonight for just a little luck.

It felt like forever driving to our spot.
I hoped that we would see a lot!

It was a long walk into the blind.
The food plot was so green
it almost shined!

We sat in our chairs, as quiet as we could.
I sat so still Dad said I was doing so good!

The first thing we saw
was a bunch of small birds.
There were so many
I was at a loss for words.

The next thing out was a couple of does.
It was so cold I couldn't feel my toes!

After a while
we could see lots of deer.
Hoping our target buck
would soon appear.

All of a sudden out
came a big buck.
He fed out front
so we were in luck!

The buck was a giant
with ten huge points.
If he ended up on our wall,
he would not disappoint.

Dad reached to pick up his bow.
His arrow was nocked and ready to go!

The buck walked in range
and turned to the side.
My dad drew his bow
and his arrow did slide.

Finger on the trigger and ready to squeeze,
I hoped he would hit his mark!
Oh please, oh please!!

Dad touched off the release
and let the arrow fly!
Right behind the shoulder,
the buck will die.

The buck ran as fast as a car!
We saw him go down, he didn't go far.

Dad was so happy as we loaded the truck. The deer was a giant it was his biggest buck!

As we got to the house, Mom came to see, too. Mom said, "Honey, I'm so proud of you!"

Hunting with Dad, I really learned a lot!
Next time, hopefully I take the shot!

Words To Know

Food Plot - an area planted with food to attract and feed wildlife.

Buck - A male deer. Bucks have antlers on their heads unlike female deer (doe).

Nock - a plastic piece at the end of an arrow that attaches the arrow to the bowstring.

Release -a device that attaches to the bow's string and helps the archer pull the string back and release it.

Deer Hunting with Dad

Deer Hunting with Dad Quiz

1) While in the deer blind what part of Hank's body became very cold?

_____

2) How many points did Hank's Dad's buck have?

_____

3) How did you feel when Dad harvested his biggest buck?

_____

f Follow us on Facebook for your chance to win free hunting and outdoor gear!

Hank's Activity Page!
Word Search

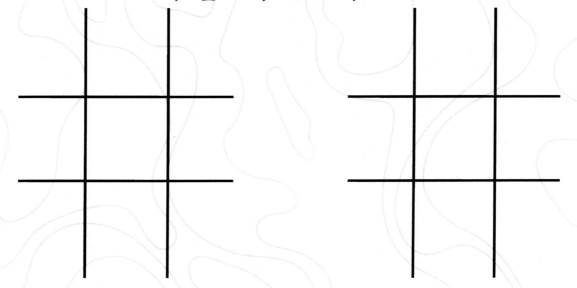

```
W Z L A B F J Z B G K H
W W E N P B Q S W R A O
O U T D O O R S M A N M
K J I Y D U R D D I S F
H B T R E E S T A N D H
A N O T E D T A D D E Z
N G O W R P Z U A S T T
K F O C A Q D W A W K H
T B U C K P D E N Z Q R
B L I N D O L A U F I O
B Z B G O E S O I G Y M
X H D F R U V K T Y R Z
```

HANK
OUTDOORSMAN
DEER
FOOD
PLOT
TREESTAND
RELEASE
BUCK
BOW
BLIND
DAD
NOCK

Tik - Tac - Toe

Made in the USA
Middletown, DE
19 October 2022

13103957R00015